DANGER EYES

This edition first published in Great Britain in 1999
First published in Great Britain 1995 by Mammoth
an imprint of Egmont Children's Books Limited
239 Kensington High Street, London W8 6SA.
Mammoth paperback edition first published 1995.
Published in hardback by Heinemann Library,
a division of Reed Educational and Professional Publishing Limited
by arrangement with Egmont Children's Books Limited.
Text copyright © Jon Blake 1995
Illustrations copyright © Nick Sharratt 1995
Additional illustrations copyright © Nick Sharratt 1999
The Author and Illustrator have asserted their moral rights.
Paperback ISBN 0 7497 3779 4
Hardback ISBN 0 431 06187 4
10 9 8 7 6 5 4 3 2 1
A CIP catalogue record for this title
is available from the British Library.
Printed at Oriental Press Limited, Dubai.

Jon Blake

DANGER EYES

Illustrated by
Nick Sharratt

 YELLOW BANANAS

To Millie and George

N.S.

Chapter One

ONE EVENING A cat arrived at our window and we decided to let it in. Dad was not in at the time, which was a good thing. Dad liked to see everything in its place and would soon notice an extra cat.

The cat sat on top of the telly and scanned the room. It had an unusually high forehead and eyes like glassy green marbles.

5

First, it stared at Mum, then at my brother
Mark, then at me. My name is Claire. Usually
I like cats, but there was something about this
one which disturbed me. After a few seconds,
I turned my eyes away.

Dad came home in an angry mood that night.
Someone had stolen the wing-mirror from his
car. He ranted and raved and chased the
strange cat into the yard.

Later that night we were woken by a clatter.

'That cat's in again,' said Mum.

'I'll see to it,' said Dad.

Dad stormed off down the stairs. Things went
quiet for a while, then the back door slammed.
Soon my bedroom door opened and the cat
walked in.

I went to the window. Dad was sitting
outside in the pouring rain.

Next morning, Dad couldn't see what the fuss
was about. 'I often sit outside at night,' he said.

'Alan,' said Mum, 'I really don't think you do.'

'I know my own mind,' said Dad.

Dad said nothing about the cat, which was

now asleep on his favourite cardigan. He put on his suit, and went off to work. Dad always went to work at exactly 9.55 am, and  he came home at precisely 6.45 pm. Today, however, he was back at 1.21 pm, and a strange smell came with him.

'It's coming from the pocket of your suit,' said Mum.

'I know where it's coming from,' said Dad.

Dad put his hand in his pocket and pulled out a piece of raw fish.

'Ugh!' said Mum. 'It's a cod's head!'

'I know what it is,' said Dad.

Dad fed the cod's head to the cat and went back to work without another word.

By now we were quite worried about Dad, but worse was to come.

Chapter Two

THE NEXT DAY was Saturday, and Mum gave Dad a shopping-list:

2 pints semi-skimmed milk
1 loaf nutty brown bread
200g medium Irish cheddar
3 large Spanish onions

'You won't forget anything, will you, love?' said Mum.

'I'm not a complete idiot,' said Dad.

Half an hour later Dad was back. 'There you go,' he said. 'Twelve tins of Katto Supermeat, one packet of Fishy Go-Crunch, a ball of wool and a scratching pole.'

'Alan,' said Mum, 'these are not what I wanted.'

'I beg your pardon!' said Dad, holding up the list. 'Here it is in black and white!'

Mum read the list again:

2 pints semi-skimmed milk

1 loaf nutty brown bread

200g medium Irish cheddar

3 large Spanish onions

'Perhaps you'd better have a lie down, love,' she said.

Later that day, Dad disappeared completely. Mum decided to call Mark and me to a meeting.

'I'm afraid your dad is going downhill fast,' said Mum.

'What's wrong with him?' I asked.

'Search me,' said Mum.

'What shall we do about it?' asked Mark.

'Haven't a clue,' said Mum.

'So why are we having this meeting?' I asked.

'Good question,' said Mum.

Suddenly there was a howl from Mark. He pointed shakily at the French windows. Dad was standing outside, holding a dead mouse by the tail.

Dad rapped on the window till the cat woke up, then waved the mouse excitedly.

'Open up!' shouted Dad.

'You're not coming in here with that thing!' shrieked Mum.

'I can't lay the table in the yard!' huffed Dad.

At this point I took Mark quietly to one side. 'I think we'd better go and see the Wilby Sisters,' I whispered.

Chapter Three

THE WILBY SISTERS had a tree-house, where they kept watch over the life of the gardens.

Emily was the oldest. She was a calm, serious person who had an infra-red telescope. Sometimes she stayed up all night, watching the nests, the burrows and the meeting-places.

Annie was the youngest. She was a nervy, funny person who could imitate all the animals. She kept all the information about the local wildlife on a computer. She knew the weight of every wood louse, the pedigree of every pet and the length of every worm.

If anyone knew about a new cat in the neighbourhood, it would be the Wilby Sisters.

'I hope they're in,' I said, as we climbed the ladder to the tree-house.

'They're never out,' said Mark.

Mark was right. The Wilby Sisters were busy as usual. The tree-house was a mess of tea-cups, sleeping-bags and computer print-out paper. Emily and Annie welcomed us up and told us the news.

'Dogfight at number 12,' said Emily calmly.

'Blue-tits nesting at 30,' said Annie nervously.

'Six snails squashed under number 2's wheelbarrow,' they chorused.

I described the cat which had invaded our home.

'Did it look like this?' asked Annie. She suddenly went stiff, with her eyebrows up and her eyes as round as plates.

'Yes, that's the one,' said Mark.

'We've had our eye on that one,' said Emily.

Annie tapped a few keys on the computer, and the new cat's details came up on the

screen. The Wilby Sisters had traced its every step.

I described what had happened to Dad. The Wilby Sisters were not surprised in the least.

'We know exactly what's the matter with your

dad,' said Emily.

'Yes?' we said eagerly.

'Hypnotised!' said Annie.

I couldn't believe it. 'Hypnotised?' I gasped.
'By a cat?'

The Wilby Sisters nodded.

'Cats can't hypnotise!' scoffed Mark.

'This one can,' replied Emily.

'Don't tell me,' I said. 'It's really an alien from
outer space.'

'No, no, no!' said Annie. 'This is a normal cat.
All the other cats are aliens from outer space.'

'That's why they can't hypnotise,' added
Emily.

'I think I get you,' I replied.
All I was really getting was
a headache.

Chapter Four

MUM WAS NOT impressed by the Wilby Sisters'
advice. Like most grown-ups, she thought the
Wilby Sisters should live in a normal home and
stop being peculiar.

'That's rubbish!' she said. 'Tonight, as a test, I
shall lock myself in the room with it all night.'

Mum did just that. In the morning, fearing the
worst, I knocked on the door. Mum opened it,
looking much the same as she did every
morning.

'Are you all right, Mum?' I asked.

'Of course I'm all right,' said Mum.

'How about the cat?' I asked.

'Perfectly normal,' said Mum. 'But don't call her "the cat".'

'What should I call her?' I asked.

'By her name,' said Mum, impatiently.

'What name?' I asked, nervously.

'Fluffington Spencer the Third,' replied Mum.

'Fluffington Spencer the Third?' I gasped. 'What kind of a name is that?'

'The name she has chosen!' snapped Mum, even more impatiently.

At that moment I happened to glance past Mum into the room. The cat was sitting on a golden cushion with a string of pearls round her neck.

'OK, Mum,' I said. I closed the door gently and went to find Mark. 'I think we're on our own now, Mark.' I said.

Mark and I made up some rules to guard us from the cat. First, we were never to talk about the cat where she could hear us. We were never to say 'the cat', and certainly not 'Fluffington Spencer the Third'. We were to call her by her code name, FS3. Most importantly, we were to keep our eyes on the ceiling, which was the one place FS3 never walked.

Unfortunately, Mark is not a very responsible person. He said the rules made his neck ache. He invented a new rule, called 'Mark's rule', which said that Mark could do as he liked. So what if FS3 stared at him? Mark would simply stare back. We would soon see who had the stronger brain.

A couple of days later, Mark came into my room with his fist raised high. 'I won!' he declared.

Mark described the staring match he'd had with FS3.

'How do you know you won?' I asked.

'Because,' said Mark, 'I'm not hypnotised.'

'But how do you know you're not hypnotised?' I asked.

'Because,' said Mark, 'I'm normal.'

'But how do you know you're normal?' I asked.

'Because,' he snapped, 'I can do woodwork!'

This seemed a strange thing to say. Mark had never shown any interest in wood before. I feared the worst.

For the next hour, the house was filled with the sounds of banging and sawing. Eventually I could stand it no more. I went downstairs to investigate.

Mark was in the hall. His tools were by the back door.

'Done,' he said, proudly.

I looked closely at the door.

At the bottom of it was a cat-flap.

On the cat-flap were the words:

FLUFFINGTON SPENCER THE THIRD: FOR THE PERSONAL USE OF.

It was all down to me now.

Chapter Five

DAYS PASSED AND the house got madder. Dad took whole mornings off to tickle FS3's chin.

Mark got up in the middle of the night to rewind the clockwork mouse.

Mum spent hours in the garden, building FS3 a pyramid.

I kept my eyes on the ceiling and said nothing. I knew that FS3 was just biding her time. She would wait till I least expected it, then she would strike.

I needed help. That meant another visit to the Wilby Sisters.

Chapter Six

ANNIE AND EMILY greeted me like a long-lost daughter. They'd seen what had happened to Mark and Mum. They feared I'd gone the same way.

I told them about the rules I'd made up with Mark, and how I always kept my eyes on the ceiling.

'Isn't that difficult?' asked Annie.

'Very difficult,' I replied. 'Especially when you're cutting your toenails.'

'You can't keep it up forever,' said Emily.

I agreed. FS3 was sure to catch my eye sooner or later. My biggest fear was that she would creep up from behind, and take me by surprise.

'What you need,' said Emily, 'is wing-mirrors.'

'Wing-mirrors?' I said. 'I'm not a car!'

'Emily's right,' said Annie. 'Wing-mirrors are the only answer.'

I thought about it. 'But I don't know how to make them,' I said.

'You'll find a way,' said Emily.

I began to panic. 'Can't you come down and help me?' I pleaded.

Annie and Emily sadly shook their heads.

They explained about all the work they had to do, and how they couldn't possibly leave the tree-house. FS3 was not the only problem in the gardens.

'I'll never beat FS3 on my own!' I cried.

Emily reached out with a hand like an old bird's claw, and took hold of my shoulder. Though her face was wrinkled, her eyes were as fierce and bright as any animal's. 'Claire,' she said. 'You will beat FS3.'

Emily seemed very certain. Half of me believed her. Half of me wasn't so sure.

Chapter Seven

LATE THAT AFTERNOON, I found two handbag mirrors, and taped them onto ballpoint pens. Then I fixed the mirrors-and-pens either side of my headphones. Now I had wing-mirrors, and what was more, they worked.

I wore my wing-mirrors in the house.

I wore them out in the garden.

I even wore them down to the shops.

They made me feel much more confident. I
could see forwards, sideways and backwards.
I could see FS3 coming a mile away.

At first, Mum and Dad didn't say anything
about my wing-mirrors. They were so involved
with looking after FS3, they hardly noticed I
was in the house. One day, however, their
attitude suddenly changed.

Claire,' said Mum, 'I think it's time you
took that ridiculous contraption
off your head.'

'Why?' I asked.

'Because . . .' said Dad.

'I'm not going to,'
I replied.

There was a tense silence. I was sure Mum and Dad were going to give me a good telling-off, but they said nothing.

Later that evening, we were all sitting in the living-room. Mark was watching telly, Dad was snoozing in the chair, and Mum was doing the crossword. It almost seemed like a normal evening. Suddenly, without a word, exactly at the same time, all three of them stood up.

One after the other, they left the room. Mum went upstairs, Mark went down the hall, and Dad went into the kitchen.

A door slammed shut. Then another. Then another. A key turned. Then another. Then another.

I decided to go into the hall to investigate. Just as I got there, Mark swooped past me, and locked the living-room door. Still without a word, Mum, Dad and Mark went out of the front door, and locked that as well.

All too late, I saw that I was trapped.

Chapter Eight

DOWN THE HALLWAY, the cat-flap rattled.

A paw came through.

Then a head.

Then the rest of FS3.

Our eyes met. In that second, all the rules went clean out of my head. Her eyes were like still, green pools, and I was slowly, slowly, sinking.

'Give in,' said a ghostly voice. 'Give in, Claire.'

I was giving in, but then somehow, from somewhere, there came another voice, 'Fight, Claire!' it said. 'Fight!'

With one last desperate effort, I broke off a
wing-mirror and held it to FS3's face.

In a matter of moments, FS3 had hypnotised
herself.

'Sleep,' I said. Her eyes closed.

'Wake,' I said. Her eyes opened.

'Take your spell off everyone in this house,' I
said, 'and never hypnotise us again!'

Sure enough, later that day, Mum, Dad and

Mark were completely back to normal. I
explained what had happened, and showed
them the cat-flap, the pyramid and the seventy-
three tins of Katto Supermeat.

Everyone laughed and laughed.

'Here's ten pounds,' said Mum.

'Buy whatever you want,' said Dad.

I set off for the shops, picturing battenburg, chocolate eclairs, and raspberry ripple ice-cream. As I passed the front window, I happened to see FS3, lazily cleaning her ears. What a harmless, lovable pussycat she seemed. It was hard to believe what she had put us through. Still, that was all behind us now.

Half an hour later I was back. 'There you go,'
I said. 'Three bags of giblets, a quarter of
catnip, and twelve more tins of Katto
Supermeat.'

Mum and Dad's faces dropped.

'Only joking,' I said.

Or was I?

The End

Yellow Bananas are bright, funny, brilliantly imaginative stories written by some of today's top writers. All the books are beautifully illustrated in full colour.

So if you've enjoyed this story, why not pick another from the bunch?

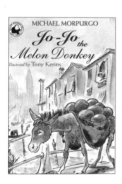

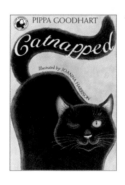